SCARY TALES RETOLD™

TEN MISSING PRINCESSES

by Wiley Blevins • illustrated by Steve Cox

RED CHAIR PRESS

Please visit our website at **www.redchairpress.com** for more high-quality products for young readers.

About the Author

Wiley Blevins has taught elementary school in both the United States and South America. He has also written over 70 books for children and 15 for teachers, as well as created reading programs for schools in the U.S. and Asia with Scholastic, Macmillan/McGraw-Hill, Houghton Mifflin Harcourt, and other publishers. Wiley currently lives and writes in New York City.

About the Artist

Steve Cox lives in Bath, England. He first designed toys and packaging for other people's characters. But he decided to create his own characters and turned full time to illustrating. When he is not drawing books he plays lead guitar in a rock band.

Publisher's Cataloging-In-Publication Data

Names: Blevins, Wiley. | Cox, Steve, 1961- illustrator. | Blevins, Wiley. Scary tales retold.
Title: Ten missing princesses / by Wiley Blevins ; illustrated by Steve Cox.
Other Titles: Twelve dancing princesses. English.

Description: South Egremont, MA : Red Chair Press, [2017] | Interest age level: 006-009. | Summary: "When the King asks a soldier to solve a mystery, he has no idea of the mysteries that will be discovered. Follow along and see for yourself, as the princesses dance the night away."--Provided by publisher.

Identifiers: LCCN 2016934122 | ISBN 978-1-63440-168-5 (library hardcover) | ISBN 978-1-63440-172-2 (paperback) | ISBN 978-1-63440-176-0 (ebook)

Subjects: LCSH: Princesses--Juvenile fiction. | Soldiers--Juvenile fiction. | Missing persons--Juvenile fiction. | Horror tales. | CYAC: Princesses--Fiction. | Soldiers--Fiction. | Missing persons--Fiction. | LCGFT: Fairy tales.

Classification: LCC PZ7.B618652 Te 2017 (print) | LCC PZ7.B618652 (ebook) | DDC [E]--dc23

Scary Tales Retold first published by:
Red Chair Press LLC   PO Box 333   South Egremont, MA 01258-0333

Printed in the United States of America

0617 1P CGBF17

Once in a faraway land, lived ten princesses. Each was more beautiful than the last.

The ten princesses slept in ten beds in the same room of a giant castle.

Every night, after they were tucked in, the
door was tightly locked by the king.

Yet each morning, the shoes of the princesses were worn and dirty—covered in cobwebs and smelling of freshly dug graves.

The king grew confused.

"I will offer great riches and a daughter's hand in marriage to anyone who can discover the secret of the worn shoes," he said.

Many men tried. All failed.

One day, a soldier heard of the king's problem. As he traveled to the castle, he passed an old woman in the forest.

"Take this special cloak," she said. "When you need to hide, put it on. You will become invisible. And don't eat anything the princesses give you. For it will contain a sleeping potion."

That night, knowing the soldier was
there to discover their secret, the oldest
princess offered the soldier something to
eat. But he secretly tossed it away.

Then the soldier began snoring loudly,
as if he was fast asleep.

Believing he was sleeping, the ten princesses
dressed in their finest gowns. Then they crept
through a trap door in the castle floor.

The soldier put on the special cloak and followed the princesses.

Tip. Tip. Toe. Tip. Toe. Tip.

The princesses walked into the forest and
past three large groves of trees. The first had
trees with silver leaves. The second had trees
with golden leaves. And the third had trees
with leaves of shiny diamonds.

The soldier snapped a branch from each type
of tree and hid them under his cloak.

Finally, the princesses arrived at a small lake. There ten ghostly princes with ten small boats awaited them.

The princes rowed the princesses to a castle on a hill.
The soldier waited below.

At the castle, the princesses danced all night until the sun poked its head above the horizon.

Tra-la-la. La-loo. Tra-la-la. La-lee.
Their shoes were worn and dirty.

"Hurry," said the oldest princess. "We must get home before the soldier or our father awakes."

The soldier buttoned up his cloak and followed them.

That morning the king called the soldier to come before him. "Tell me my daughters' secret," he said. "Or you will die like the other men who failed."

The soldier gathered the three tree branches
he had collected and told the king what he
had seen.

The princesses gasped and fell back in surprise.

"For solving the secret," said the king, you may
marry one of my daughters."
The soldier chose the most beautiful daughter.

On their wedding day, the princess took the
soldier into the forest. They walked past groves
of trees covered in leaves of silver, gold, and
diamonds. Then they began to dance.

But as they did, the princess turned from
a beautiful girl into a skeleton. She giggled
and twirled as the soldier desperately tried
to free himself.

It was no use.

The soldier would never leave the forest. There he remains as another ghostly prince in the castle on the hill. Waiting to dance the night away.

THE END